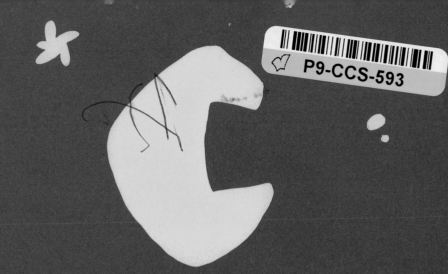

To RYAN and MEGAN
With a special thank you to AILEEN RAISTRICK

Text copyright © Vincent James 1992
Illustrations copyright © Vincent James 1992

First published in 1992 by
Hazar Publishing Ltd
147 Chiswick High Road, Chiswick, London W4 2DT
Editions Hazar, 10 Bis Avenue de L'Yser, 78800 Houilles, France

Printed and bound in Singapore
by Imago

Graphic Design by Keith Pointing Design Consultancy

ISBN: 0-681-00645-5

First Longmeadow Press Edition 1994
0987654321

MY FAVORITE

VINCENT JAMES

LONGMEADOW
P R E S S

**201 High Ridge Road
Stamford, CT. 06904**

When bedtime comes, I've heard it said,
some children check beneath the bed...

they lose their sleep, they lose their hair,
in fear of monsters lying there…

but monsters I have always found,
are lots of fun to have around.

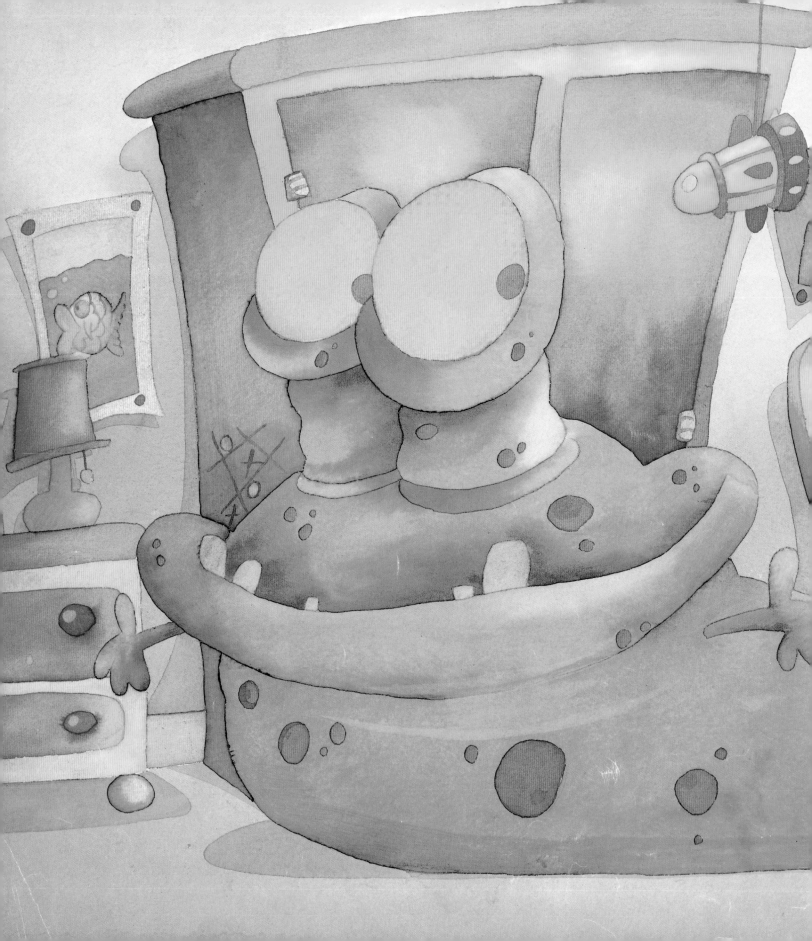

In fact there's one under my bed,
he's very friendly, his name is Ted…

and Daniel the dragon has made his lair
in my toy box over there.

In my top drawer among the socks,
lives an eight eyed 'Squengie', whose name is Jock.

In the wardrobe where it's very dim,
lives Colin but he's never in.

Outside in our garden shed,
lives a monster I call 'Spongy' Fred.

Now this monster's name is Norma Grosset,
she hides inside the linen closet.

Jim, with a face like an alligator
snuggles behind the radiator.

Lastly, there's Roger, I like him a lot,
he lives inside our old teapot.

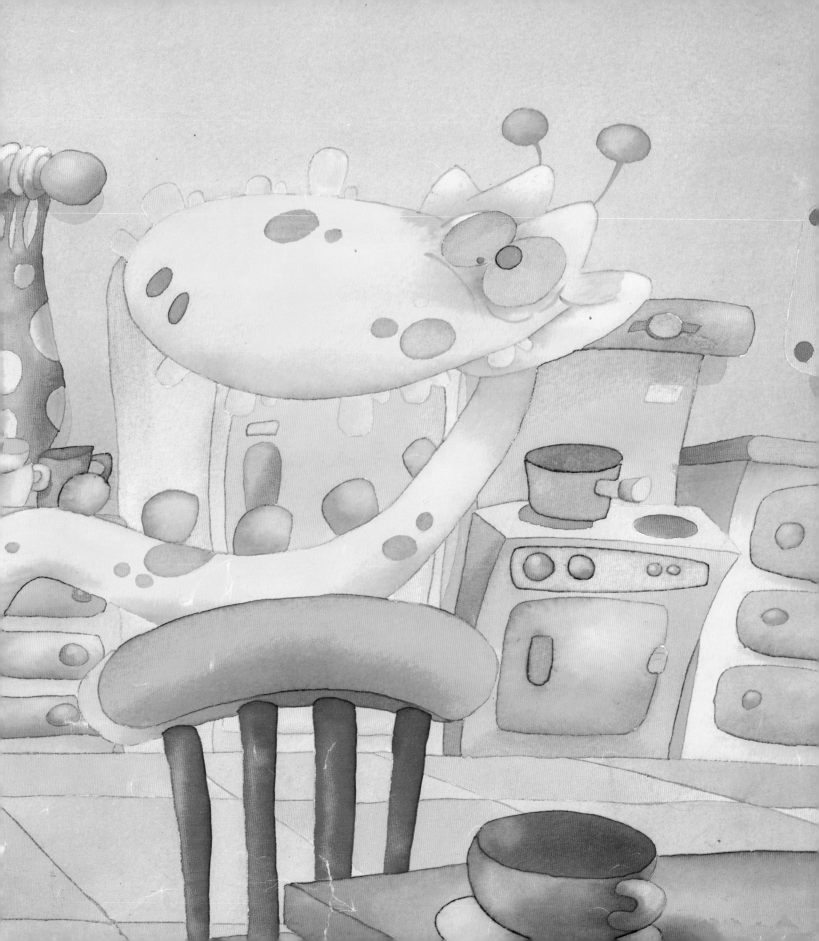

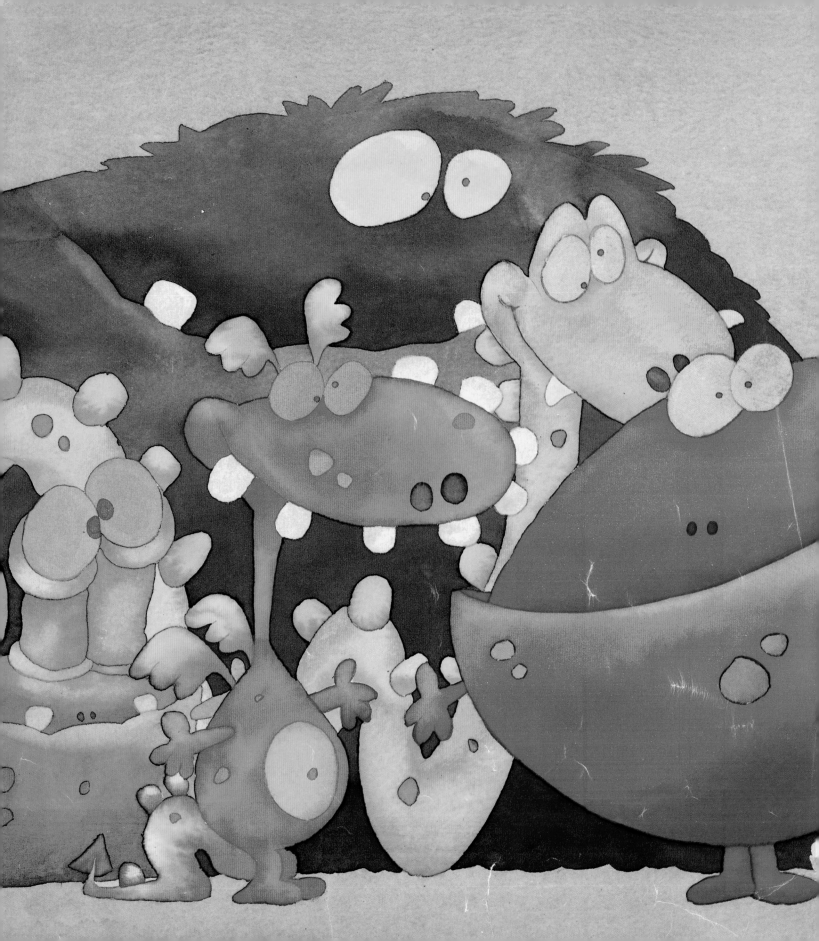

So monsters, whether big or small,
needn't frighten us at all.

Just remember to be polite,
and don't forget to say goodnight.